by

D. B. Albiza

Illustrated by

Elizabeth Quiñonez

Betty Books ♥ Miami

Cruel Nature Copyright © 2023 by Denise B. Albiza

www.bettybookspress.com

Publisher's Cataloging-in-Publication data

Names: Albiza, D. B., author. | Quiñonez, Elizabeth, illustrator.

Title: Cruel nature : seven terrifying tales to trouble your sleep. / by D. B. Albiza; illustrated by Elizabeth Quiñonez.

Description: Miami, FL: Betty Books, 2023. | Summary: Seven stories about the hidden dangers lurking in nature.

Identifiers: LCCN: 2023919874 | ISBN: 979-8-9893783-0-2 (paperback) | 979-8-9893783-1-9 (eBook)

Subjects: LCSH Nature--Juvenile fiction. | Horror stories. | Short stories. | BISAC JUVENILE FICTION / Horror | JUVENILE FICTION / Paranormal, Occult & Supernatural

Classification: LCC PZ7.1 .A53 Cr 2023 | DDC [Fic]--dc23

First Edition

To

Fred, because you never stopped believing I could do this and you love me, despite me.

Aaron and Ellie, you collaborated, edited, and held my hand through this whole journey.

Nick, you guided me through to the finish line with encouragement, earnest advice, and a marvelous sense for storytelling.

Ondina, you have always cheered me on and championed whatever I do.

My family and friends, you lifted me up and carried me through a pretty rough time.

Mom, this is from the part of me that is you. You are always in my heart.

God, who has always watched over me. I know this because he blessed me with all of the above mentioned and so much more.

Acknowledgments

Special thanks to Terry Alexander who graciously gave of her time to make sure this book was not riddled with errors.

If you shudder at the thought,
of ghosts and ghouls and things that rot.

Close this book at once and go. There are
things in these pages you should not know.

Go and read some happy tale,
Where light and good always prevail.

With cartoon lands in sherbet hues, of
cotton candy and no bad news.

But!

If a scream, in the dead of night, wraps
your heart in pure delight.

If some lore of woe and dread
as you clutch the covers on your bed

Stir in you some morbid zeal,
a ghoulish excitement you dare not reveal.

Then this, dear reader, is the book for you.
Before you read on, here's what you should do.

Lock the doors and draw the blinds.
Dim the lights. No one minds.

Listen to the rain out there
as you settle in a cozy chair.

Pay no mind to shadows in the room,
like silent mourners drawn to doom.

They've gathered 'round for a tale or two,
that curdle the blood, and so have you.

The mood is set. The time is right.
Now turn the page and let's all have a fright!

Table of Contents

The Hole

A man and his dog were out hunting in the Florida Everglades one day. The dog, a high-strung beagle named Penelope, ran off through the pinelands to an area the man had never hunted before. He followed the dog's trail deep into the thicket. He called to her several times, but she did not return to him. As he trudged through the murky water in a shallow slough, he caught sight of her trail in the mud. Her paw prints led him to a hardwood hammock. The sun was quickly slipping below the treetops. Nestled within the hammock he came upon a clearing where the dying light of day broke through the dense canopy. There, in the middle of the clearing stood a small derelict Cracker house. The little house was a ruin of ashen wood planks raised up on feet made of piled rocks. There was a crumbling chimney stack on one side and the roof was covered by fallen branches and leaves. Dust muted every surface and generations of cobwebs draped the corners beneath the roof of the porch. It was there he found Penelope furiously sniffing back and forth until she reached the front door. Suddenly, she stopped and backed away whimpering. She ran from the porch then turned and barked. By this time, it was almost completely dark and the hunter was weary from the long hike. He was experienced enough to know not to go trekking through the swamp at night. Still, something had spooked the dog and raised the hairs on the hunter's neck as well. Despite this, he felt it was best to seek shelter in the house and head back in the morning.

He offered Penelope a treat from his pocket. At the sight of it, she forgot what it was that had spooked her and ran back to the porch. Inside, the faint light filtering through a dirty window revealed a large central room where the fireplace stood. Across from the hearth at the far right corner was a door leading to a smaller room; that was the entirety of the small structure. The bare wood floor was covered in dirt and various discarded items. Old newspapers, a couple of empty cloudy mason jars, and a rusty length of twisted wire littered the floor of the main room. The man, who was used to roughing it out in the wilds, made quick work of settling in for the night. He made a fire using wood he scrounged from outside and used some of the newspaper as kindling. The chimney had collapsed a long time ago, but there was nothing to block the smoke from rising up and out. The hunter pulled a small grey squirrel out of his pack which Penelope had cornered earlier that morning. He set about skinning it and roasting it over the fire. Penelope sat intently next to the man as he prepared their food. She swiveled her head to raise one ear up. Then she swiveled back to raise the other, mindfully seesawing back and forth trying to make dog sense of human actions. At one point, she gently patted his hand with her paw, reminding him to include her in the meal. While they ate their supper of squirrel and hard tack, the hunter noticed something peculiar about the dog. Her coat seemed darker. There was less tan among her black and tan patches, and she seemed to be larger. Maybe she had rolled in the dirt to pick up a scent as beagles do. Maybe that had ruffled her fur, making it shaggier. He shrugged off the observation deciding it could also be an effect of the light from the fire. Aside from the flames, the rest of the room- indeed, the rest of the house- was as black as crow's feathers. After dinner the hunter made a crude grease lamp from an old jar and tallow he rendered from the squirrel.

As he was fashioning the lamp, he heard a faint scream from somewhere outside. He put down the jar and went to the front door. Just before he opened it, he heard another sound. This time it was a dreadful wail that stopped short. He waited for more, but there was only dead silence. He called out into the deep dark of the woods, "Hello?! Is anyone there!?" No one answered. The low symphony of crickets, frogs and other small night dwellers was eerily absent. Penelope stood next to the hunter with her tail straight as an antenna whimpering thinly, sensing something, but seeing nothing. The moon's light had been put out by a bank of clouds. Minutes passed without any noise. Penelope huffed as the hunter closed the door and they both returned to the fireside.

After a short while the hunter explored the other room of the house by the light of the grease lamp, which illuminated only a small circle around him. As he made his way through the simple structure the beagle sniffed around in and out of the light. Again, the hunter took notice of the dog and thought she seemed larger and scruffier, but it was too dark to really see as the dog was darting from room to room. Deciding he was very tired and should get some sleep the idea was quickly brushed away. Back at the fireplace a folded coat for a pillow and the dusty stone floor of the hearth served as a bed. Weary as he was, he could not fall asleep and instead lay there, looking out at the room. It was then that he noticed a hole in the wall opposite from the fire where he was laying. It was a jagged hole, no more than the size of a matchbook. Befuddled that he had not noticed it before he stared at it when cracking sounds began echoing from the hole. Rising to investigate, he caught sight of an animal the size of a small goat with rough mottled fur curled in one corner asleep with its back to him. Confused, he blinked several times to adjust his eyes. *Where was Penelope?* Again, he heard cracking and rustling from the hole. He turned his back to the creature and slowly approached the wall trying to figure out what the stirring cracking sounds could be. He placed his right eye to the hole where he was astounded by the sight of woods. He recognized it as the forest outside. This was impossible as the other side of the hole should be the small empty room on the other side of the wall. He pulled away from the hole and ran around the wall to the other side. Just as he had seen earlier, there was the empty room. He ran his hand across the wall where the other side of the hole should be. There was no hole in the wall inside the small room. The hunter felt a slow creep up his spine. *Had he imagined everything?* Walking back to the main room on the other side of the wall he found the same jagged hole. The fire was still burning but, the creature and Penelope had somehow disappeared even though the door was closed and the window was shut. A heavy sense of dread weighed in his stomach like a stone as he broke out into a cold sweat. He opened the door and called out to the beagle. Nothing happened. Then he heard quick breathing coming from the hole. He raced back to look through it and saw two dark figures hastening through the woods barely lit by moonlight. He could not tell who or what they were, but it appeared to be a chase. He could hear someone huffing and whimpering. He stepped away from the wall and began to pace back and forth. Real fear and panic began welling up inside of him. He did not understand what was happening, but something inside of him knew it was bad. Without warning, he heard a familiar voice screaming his name. It was calling to him from the hole. He lurched at the wall and fixed his eye again over the hole. In horror, he saw himself with a bloodied throat and chest completely disheveled running in a panic through the woods towards him, running towards the hole. He

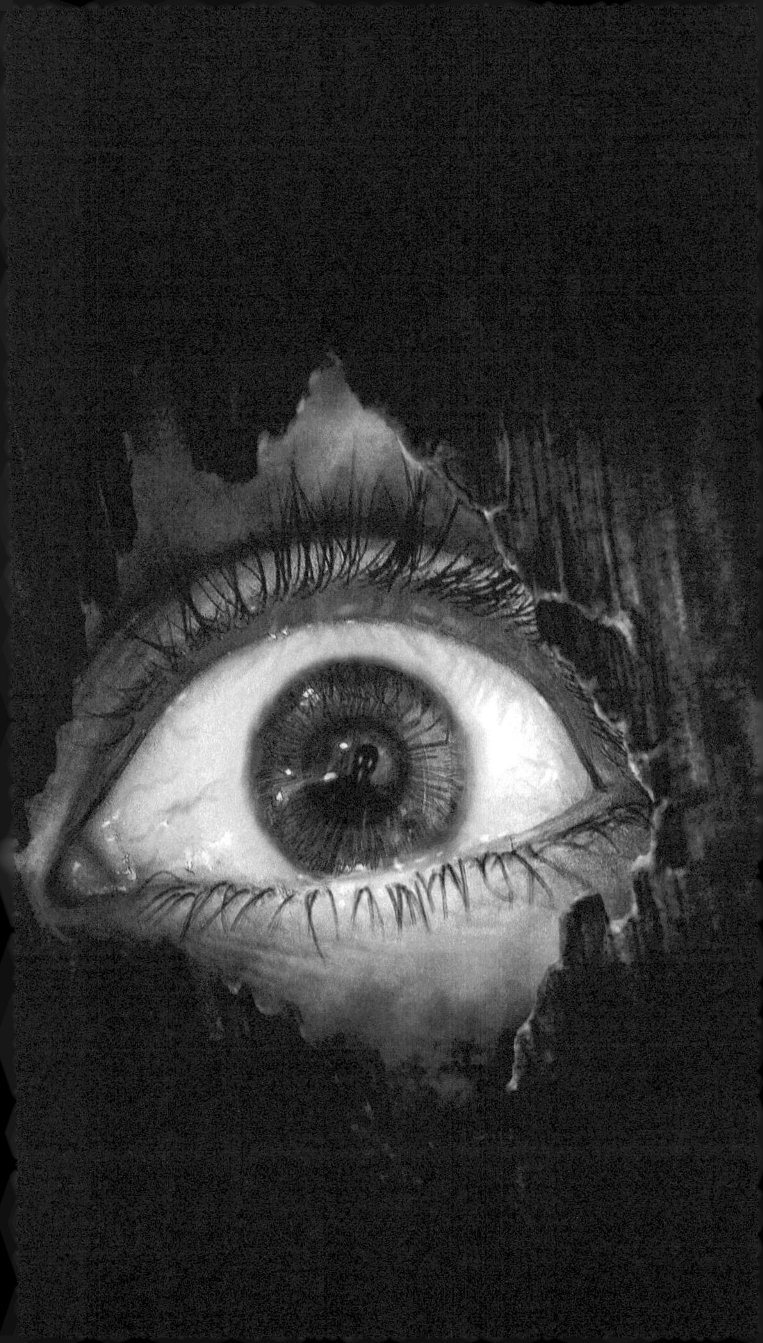

locked eyes with his other self whose face was contorted in terror. His other self screamed, "Run!" Just then the front door burst open and in bounded Penelope. Her fur was now a brindled black. Her muscles bulked to horrific proportions and her paws were gruesome clawed hands. Perched on her haunches, she was as tall as him. She sat there panting. The hunter remained frozen by a maddening disbelief and terror. Her muzzle was now a long salivating maw crammed with a jumble of bloody fangs, each impossibly long. They glistened in the fire's light as she swiveled her head up from one side to the other slowly as if to consider him. In that second a fleeting glimpse of his Penny surfaced, but the hunter's hopes were dashed as her eyes revealed no recognition of their former bond. Her eyes were now the two cold black eyes of a predator. The beast that was once Penelope the beagle rose up onto its hind legs to a towering height. She, or rather it, stopped panting and for a split second the air between them stilled. The hunter's heart beat furiously as he stood there in wait. Then the monster lunged straight at the hunter. He side stepped it narrowly missing it's teeth. He bolted out the front door and into the woods. The beast turned and chased him. They both darted over and under through the glades. At one point the monster nearly caught him by the heel. He screamed out as in the distance he could see the house. The door which should be open was closed. Just then the hunter turned to see the creature closing the distance between them. The creature reached out one long arm and caught him by the shirt collar. He wailed as he fell back then stopped short as his body made a thud on the ground. The creature clawed at the hunter's chest and throat as he wrestled to free himself. Off in the distance at the little house he saw the door open and two silhouettes appeared. He could hear his own voice yelling out, "Hello?! Is anyone there!?"

Scritchity Scratch

A thought is a bird
that lands on your head.
Sometimes it visits you
just before bed.

Without invitation,
it appears in your mind,
to tug at your fears.
It's really unkind.

As visions of sugar plums
dance in your head,
along comes a thought
to fill you with dread.

Perhaps, it's a memory
you'd rather forget,
of something you did
you truly regret.

You picked on your sister
and caused her to cry.
You broke a neighbor's window,
then told them a lie.

These thoughts are bothersome.
Yes, this is so.
Still, there are worse thoughts,
you won't want to know.

The most dreadful thought
you must never let in,
is that of an evil
so stealthy and grim.

To utter its name
will call it to you.
Once on your scent,
there's nothing you can do.

It hunts little children
and swallows them whole,
like bite-sized confections
that feed its dark soul.

Where does it come from?
Where does it dwell?
No one yet,
has lived to tell.

Surely its home
is a lair somewhere deep,
that's earthy and cold
where the tree roots sleep.

Strewn with bones
across a damp ground,
of all the poor souls
that will never be found.

It waits for its name
to arrive on the wind,
a doomed solicitation,
you cannot rescind.

Once it is beckoned
it flies through night,
with two yellow eyes
as an eerie search light.

A hideous site,
it's mouth is a flower,
of fleshy red fingers,
eager to devour.

The scent of its prey,
is a potent attraction.
It's fueled by a hunger
without satisfaction.

It moves undetected
as it makes its way thither.
It can fly, swim, and walk
and yes, even slither.

It can squeeze through a keyhole
without any care,
then rise up behind you.
You won't know it's there.

Shh! What's that?
Do you hear that sound?
A low, breathy panting
like that of a hound.

It's obvious now
that something's amiss,
there's a presence among us
you shouldn't dismiss.

While you were reading
it made its way here.
Don't you remember?
The warning was clear.

The very first words
at the top of this verse,
was the horrible name
to conjure this curse.

The Scritchity Scratch
has come for its due.
The Scritchity Scratch
has come now for YOU!

Harvester

Five children had gone missing in the small town. Cora's sister was one of them. It was late September when her sister, Charlotte and her best friend Abigail, disappeared together. The two were walking back from the Quick-mart where they had gone to buy snacks for their sleepover. The woman at the market told police that she saw the girls over by the entrance to Grady Pines, but a truck hauling a tractor drove by and blocked her view. Once it had passed, she could just make out two slender figures slipping into the forest. They were never seen again. Grady Pines was a rough triangle several acres large of wooded area that divided the town's residential neighborhoods from its main street. The land there was craggy and densely overgrown. Most people steered clear of the woodland as poison ivy grew rampant there. Still, many of the town's young folk would venture across its western tip as a shortcut to the town's main shopping district. Police and volunteers had spent a great deal of time searching the overgrown pine land, but nothing was ever found. Not a single trace of any of the five children ever emerged. A year went by and two of the families of the missing children moved away, unable to bare the memories. The rest of the families and the town shouldered forward and moved on as best they could. Since her sister's disappearance, Cora's mother had become unbearably overprotective insisting that she never be alone. Cora longed for the days from before the incident when she could freely play outside. She use to ride her bike over to the next street where her best friend Sylvia lived. Now she wasn't even allowed to play in the front yard unless someone was watching her. After the disappearances Sylvia's father took a promotion in another state, and they moved, deciding it was safer elsewhere. Cora spent all her time alone or with her mother. They began to argue more and more. A few days after the anniversary of the disappearances, Cora begged her mother to allow her to meet with a new friend from school. They planned to see a movie at the theater on Main Street. Her mother offered to drive her, but Cora pleaded to walk on her own instead. Her mother refused and Cora ran to her room to cry. It was then that her mother could see that she had been too hard on the girl. Losing Charlotte was taking a toll on their relationship. Despite her apprehension, she allowed Cora to walk to the movie theater under the one condition that she not cut through the pines. Cora was overjoyed. She agreed and raced to her room to get dressed. Just before it was time for Cora to head out, her mother reminded her that she was still responsible for bringing in and feeding the family cat. Cora called out the back door for Pumpkin, their orange tabby, but it was nowhere in sight. She called out again. Cora was getting anxious, she didn't want to be late. She checked her watch. She called a third time, and this time Pumpkin sauntered from around a potted plant on the back porch. She scooted the cat in, filled its bowl and headed for the front door where her mother stood holding out a coat she insisted Cora put on. It was late September and the evenings had taken on a crisp chill. Cora pulled on the parka and scurried out the door and down the street. She looked down the sidewalk which seemed to stretch on forever before the turn to Main Street. If she followed the street, she was guaranteed to be late, but if she cut across the tip of Grady Pines she would have about five minutes to spare. An antsy feeling came over her. She knew that she had promised not to enter the woods. The pine lands were off-limits. Then a voice inside her chimed in. *She was sure it would be fine. Her mother would never know and it had been a year since anything had happened. There was no proof that the five children had even gone missing in the woods.* That seemed to settle the matter and Cora took a hard right into the pines. It was thicker and craggier then she remembered. Over the last year the path all the kids use to tread had grown over making it harder to find the way through. It was quieter as well. Cora herself hadn't stepped foot in the pines since the summer of that nightmare year. In the summer, the woods were teaming with sounds. In the dense cold air of Autumn, the forest had grown silent. The woods seemed unfamiliar and foreboding. In the past there was always the chance that you'd run into other kids taking the shortcut. Now everyone stayed away. Cora had not considered that and began to regret her decision. She stopped and stood for a moment. She thought of going back the way she came, but then she would really be late. She was stuck and had to continue on. Cora had only been walking again for a few minutes when she heard her name being called. Turning to look in the direction of the voice she was shocked to see her sister's face poke through a bush. A small scream escaped her. She ran up to the bush which was very densely packed. In the gloom of dusk her sister's face appeared strange. It was pale and dirty. Her hair must be slicked back because she could not see her sister's long blond locks. She almost seemed bald. A broad unnatural smile stretched across her uncanny face. Her teeth were yellowed as though she hadn't brushed them the whole time she'd been gone and her open staring eyes exhibited a creepy eagerness. Cora's excitement at seeing her sister faded giving way to a sinking feeling but, she could not understand why. She asked her where she'd been all this time. Charlotte, recounted a story about a delightful place that she and the other kids had stumbled upon in a hidden cave near the center of the pines. She assured her that it was the most enchanting place. Charlotte claimed she had spent the last year doing all kinds of amusing things. She said there was no school, no chores, and no adults to order them around. She said that there were lots of kids there. She invited Cora to come with her. Then they could play together all the time. Cora sensed an eerie difference between the words that were coming out of Charlotte's mouth and her face as she said them. There was a split second delay between her voice and her pale lips. The quality of the sound was strange as well. *What was it?* It was hollow. It was Charlotte's face and voice, but Cora could feel an incongruity. And there was something else. Charlotte had not aged in a year. How was that even possible? She needed more information. Cora asked about Abigail. Charlotte, still wide eyed agreed to go fetch her. Then her face disappeared into the bush. Cora heard the rustle of leaves and something else that sounded like someone loudly cracking their knuckles. A few moments later, Abigail's face poked through. Again, the face was the same as Abigail's face but somehow not. She too was waxlike with grimy teeth and no sight of her red curls. At once Abigail began to prattle on about the magical place they found. There was a slight and almost imperceptible echo to her voice. Cora was also struck by the fact that Abigail hadn't even asked about her grandmother whom everyone knew Abigail loved most of all. It occurred to Cora as well that Charlotte didn't bother to ask how their mother was. Cora interrupted Abigail and asked for Charlotte. Abigail simply stopped talking, closed her eyes and slipped back into the bush. Cora thought that was rather odd. Abigail seemed almost mechanical. Then there was the cracking knuckles sound again. Cora didn't know why but it made her stomach sour. A minute later back popped Charlotte. Cora was happy to see her. Despite her appearance Cora realized just how much she missed her sister now that she was speaking to her. Cora felt a swell of emotion. Her nagging concerns gave way to the other intense feelings Cora had been holding inside for a year. Their mother would be so happy. She was happy. She had her sister back. She could be the one to bring them all back. Tears clouded her eyes. Cora beckoned Charlotte to come out from the bush and come hug her. Charlotte's face went blank for a second then reanimated into a reply. She explained that she and Abigail didn't have any coats so the bush was keeping them warm. Cora immediately lurched forward to offer her coat to her sister. Just then the parka caught on a low branch nearby. She tripped and fell to the ground at the base of the bush. She looked up and caught sight of something strange past the base of the trunk. There were two sets of large pointed bundles made of twisted tree roots and twigs. She could not comprehend what she was looking at. As she rose up slowly the pointed bundles moved. She stood there in front of the bush. Her sister was gone. "Charlotte?" she said. There was no reply. Then the cracking of bones and Charlotte poked through. Charlotte said nothing. She only grinned, eyes wide like those of a ventriloquist's dummy. Cora had only focused on her sister and Abigail's faces. Her eyes scanned the bush. Through holes here and there she could see the bundles of branches and vines ending in points that appeared to be attached to something larger also made of matter from the forest. It shifted slightly. What Cora did not see was feet. Charlotte's feet were missing. Cora felt a wave of nausea. She asked her sister to stick out her foot. Charlotte said nothing. Then one sharp bundle pierced through the bush at Cora scraping past her hand leaving a deep cut. She stumbled back and screamed in horror. The rest of it came through the bush almost splitting it in half. It was a huge hunching creature. It's body and four spindly legs appeared to be made of branches, bark and vines. Where its own face should be there was a grotesque collection of faces. Charlotte, Abigail, and the three other

missing children's faces were somehow monstrously grafted to the creature's head. It switched the faces around like some dreadful dial making that repulsive bone cracking sound as it shifted. Charlotte's face was still in use by the creature. The other children's faces remained expressionless in wait like masks at a Halloween shop. Cora stood frozen by the incredulous sight. Charlotte's face shrieked loud inhuman sounds that reverberated through Cora's body. She snapped out of her momentary daze and bolted through the woods. The creature cried out through Charlotte's puppeteered mouth and awkwardly galloped after Cora. Cora ran for her life hopping over tree roots and ducking under branches. Whenever it was close enough the creature would try to stab at her with one of its front legs. Just before they reached the entrance into Grady Pines from Main Street the creature managed to poke through the bottom of Cora's parka. It yanked her and she fell back hard onto the ground. The creature pinned her coat down with one leg and reared up with the other ready to pounce down on her. Frantically Cora wriggled free from the coat and scurried to her feet as the creature stabbed the empty coat. She took off and it followed her all the way to the edge of the opening that lead to Main street. It was careful not to let itself be seen by anyone else. Cora stopped just outside to catch her breath. She looked back at the entrance to the woods. She could no longer see the many-faced creature. It slipped back into the thick foliage of the bushes. She ran all the long way home. As unbelievable as the tale that Cora told them was, the police and volunteers combed over Grady Pines for days. Despite their efforts, they found nothing. Weeks after Cora's harrowing encounter, a man fishing downstream from Grady pines noticed what looked like a group of masks caught in a cluster of reeds at the river's edge. Curious, he motored over to the spot where he made a gruesome discovery. It was the faces of the five missing children floating on the water.

Horde Sweet Horde

The fall from the window on the second floor and several failed attempts to wriggle free had left Henry spent. He was also slightly concussed. He had just begun to sink into sleep when he felt a gentle tap on the fabric of his pant leg and then another on his shirt. It was rain he thought to himself as he continued to drift, eyes closed. Then he felt movement, more taps and something like nibbling. He opened his eyes in horror. It was not rain.

What was once a no man's land of abandoned houses and empty lots, was now buzzing with the sounds of construction crews and landscapers. A new factory had opened across town and with it came many new families to the area. The dormant streets were awakening. Henry, who worked at the factory had snatched up a small Victorian house next to a large empty corner lot. The house that had once stood on it was leveled years ago after it was declared a hazard. Henry, who imagined the solitude of having an empty parcel of land next to him, overlooked the waist high weeds, litter, and debris from the demolition. It pleased him to have only one neighbor to share a fence with at the rear of his property. Henry's block was long but narrow, only two houses wide to be precise. This meant that Henry had no neighbor directly on either side. He took comfort in the fact that he would not have to make small talk with anyone in the morning as he left for work or whenever he was out in the yard. The houses across the street were tucked further back on their lots and a row of trees on both sides of the streets provided ample screening. Henry could move freely about his property without any social interaction. Before Henry moved in, he meticulously cleaned the house from top to bottom. He would not put so much as a spoon away before scrubbing every inch of the place.

On the day after Henry moved in he was walking along the side of the house by the empty lot. In his arms were a stack of boxes he was planning to deposit in the trash pile on the curb. He noticed a popsicle wrapper on the ground near the fence. The wind had most likely picked it up and deposited it in his yard. Henry carefully crouched down to pick-up the wrapper, while keeping the boxes steady. Just then, a large roach that had been underneath it nibbling the sugary residue scurried up his arm. Startled, Henry quickly snatched back his hand, lost his balance and fell back onto his backside. The boxes flew into the air landing all around him. Henry shot up and frantically patted himself down searching for the roach but, it had disappeared. He straightened himself then carefully stacked the boxes again and walked them the rest of the way to the curb. He put the boxes down and looked back toward his house to admire all that he had done to the little house. He had added flower boxes under the windows, trimmed the walkway and strung lights in the back patio. He looked over to the empty lot. He saw a paper cup stranded in the weeds. He didn't want the wind to carry it to his side so he walked over to pick it up. He reached down to grab the cup and a quartet of cockroaches ran out from inside and scattered into the weeds. Henry recoiled in disgust. He looked around for any trace of more pests. He had only ever looked at the lot from his side of the wooden fence, but now that he was standing in the lot he was able to truly ascertain just how much junk, garbage, and overgrowth there was. The whole area was a paradise for pests and vermin. Henry looked around to said pests and vermin which he was sure were watching him from their collective hiding places.

"Pack your bags fellas. I'll have an exterminator out here soon." he said emphatically. With that he walked back to his side.

That night Henry couldn't sleep. He padded down the stairs. The full moon through the kitchen windows cast just enough light for Henry to make his way around. As he approached the kitchen he saw what looked like a dark brown artichoke on the counter. He hadn't bought any artichokes at the grocers when he did the shopping earlier. He stood there looking at it from the doorway. Its leaves were moving or rather vibrating in place. He watched it, mesmerized for a moment or two. His brain was trying to figure the mechanics of it, to place it with something he had seen already and known to be true. But, nothing came to mind that satisfied him. He could not make out what he was seeing. He flicked on the light and a clot of cockroaches fled from the surface of a peach he'd left on the countertop. They had scraped the skin almost completely off and were working their way through the soft flesh of the fruit. A primitive feeling of disgust made his skin crawl. He caught sight of one of the runners that had slipped into a pile of junk mail further down on the counter. He balled his hand into a fist then slammed it down, smooshing the roach between a restaurant coupon and a flyer for *Dr. Death Pest Control*. The yellow goop of the roach's innards had spewed all over the advert. He smirked at the irony. Henry picked up the postcard by one corner holding it out and away from his body. He walked over to the sink and grabbed a rag. He wiped off the roach guts and stuck the postcard to the refrigerator door using a plastic pineapple magnet. He would call them first thing in the morning.

He shuffled up the stairs and slipped back into his bed. Some time had passed and Henry was in a shallow state of sleep when he heard a crinkling noise. He recognized it as the sound of something crawling on a paper bag. He knew it must be a roach, but the undertow of sleep was pulling him down quickly. The sound was coming from across the room. It must be in the waste can he kept by his desk. As long as it stayed in its corner he was fine. With that last dwindling thought he sank into a deep sleep. In his dream, Henry was running. He was in his pajamas running towards the front door of his house in the middle of the night. Something was chasing him and he was terrified. His body moved in long rapid sprints, but he couldn't close the distance between himself and the door. No matter how much he ran the door was the same distance away. He turned to look back and a giant dark mass like a huge blob was gaining on him. The blob was made up of thousands of small crawling creatures. He looked back to the door and then as if someone pressed fast forward he was at the door, but just before he dashed in, his arm was caught on something. It was a protruding nail in the door frame. It cut into his arm. The pain stung. Just then he opened his eyes and woke up. The pain in his arm was still there. Henry was laying on his side. He could feel something poking the arm he was laying on. He figured he must have fallen asleep on something. Maybe it was his glasses. Still groggy, he slipped his other hand between his arm and the bed to retrieve whatever thing was poking him. Henry, who was terribly nearsighted, had to hold the thing right up to his face in order to make out the details of what is was. He was eye to compound eye with a large roach. Its two antennae spinning round like twin whirligigs feeling for cues. It had been trapped under his arm, in his bed, with him for a good portion of the night. Henry screamed, sat up, and flung the roach across the room. The roach took flight and swooped down towards Henry's head. Henry tumbled out of bed and kept low to the ground. He reached under his bed for one of his slippers. He slid it out from underneath and as he did so a handful of roaches scattered out from the slipper in several directions, one of which was up his arm. Henry swatted the pests away, grabbed his glasses from atop the nightstand, and yowled as he quickly crawled to his desk. He tucked himself underneath it and cautiously surveyed the room. The roaches were congregating across from him around his bed and dresser. There were dozens of roaches on the walls, along the tops of the dresser mirror, and his bed. Some flew around the room like guard helicopters scanning below for an escaped prisoner. His upper arm still stung. He felt it with his fingers. The roach had chewed through his sleeve and opened a small hole in his arm. He thought of the peach and the many pockmarks in its flesh. His stomach lurched forward and he cupped his mouth to hold back the urge to vomit. He settled himself for a moment then thought of a plan. He slowly reached up to grab the telephone on top of the desk never once looking away from the roaches. Surely they could see him, but they seemed to be waiting. For what, he did not want to find out. He carefully lowered the phone onto his lap. He placed the receiver to his ear. All he could

hear was frenzied scratching. He felt a tickle in his ear that sent a sickening tingle down his spine. He looked at the receiver. A tuft of antennae stuck out from the ear holes and side seam of the plastic receiver. Henry chucked the whole phone to the center of the room. In the seconds during which his focus was on the phone, the horde had grown into the hundreds. It was a horrifying teeming mass that moved under the direction of a single mind. He stood up from under the desk poised to run but, the horde blocked his bedroom door.   His eyes roamed over the vibrating throng of leathery brown nightmares in horror. He scanned around the room frantically. The window behind him was the only way out. The horde seemed to understand this as well and began to crowd around him. Before they could cut him off, Henry dove through the window, glass and all.

When Henry came to, his head throbbed with pain. He tried to lift a hand, but he couldn't move. He had somehow tangled himself in the string lights on the patio which had no doubt helped to lessen the blow from the fall. Henry's recollection came back like the flicker of a fluorescent light turning on. The bedroom. The roaches. He was trying to escape the horde of roaches. How long had he been out? Where are they now? Panicked, he wriggled and squirmed trying to free himself, but it was no use. He laid there on his back trying to think of a way to free himself. The sound of his own heart beating flooded his head.

He called out, "Help!" "Can anyone help me?" "I fell and I need help!"

There was no reply. No cavalry to the rescue. No friendly neighbor peeking over the fence to answer his distress call. He laid there, tangled and vulnerable. He looked up at the sky and all around the patio. The world around him was a blur of shapes and colors. He had lost his glasses during the fall. He couldn't move and he couldn't see. He laid there considering his predicament. He was covered in cuts and bruises. A shallow pulse of pain continued to beat at his head. He closed his eyes. The fall from the window and several failed attempts to wriggle free had left Henry spent. He was also slightly concussed. He had just begun to sink into sleep when he felt a gentle tap on the fabric of his pant leg and then another on his shirt. It was rain, he thought to himself as he continued to drift, eyes closed. Then he felt movement, more taps and something like nibbling. He opened his eyes. It was not rain.

Roaches, first by the handful, then more dropped or fluttered down from the window above. He lifted his head to look down the length of his body. It was covered by roaches, blurry roaches. They scurried all over him as he lay there at their mercy. Some began to slip into the folds of his clothes. He could feel their prickly legs across his skin. He twitched and writhed in protest and repulsion. His eyes darted from side to side. More brown blurs dropped from above and he could vaguely make out a trail in almost military formation marching toward him from the empty lot. Soon they were all over him moving freely in and out of his clothes. Clusters gathered at every wound site drawn by the salty taste of blood. Strangely there were no roaches on his face or head. A gruesome thought dawned on him that they wanted him to see, to prolong the torment. He was covered up to the neck now. His whole body a chittering swarm, a live wire of agony.

Then, as if on some cue, they began to devour him whole. Hundreds of roaches, nipping and gnawing through fabric and flesh. Maddened, he screamed. It was a call to action. They swarmed his head and face. They crawled into his open wailing mouth, choking him as they squeezed down into his throat and beyond.

Beneath the Ceiba

A man was out walking one hot summer day when he made a split second decision in the heat of the midday sun to switch from his usual route. He was drawn to the cool shade of a trail that ran beneath a canopy of tall trees which grew along a graveyard. It was so hot outside that no one else was out and about, not even the birds. Every other living thing had the good sense to shelter from the scorch of the sun. As he made his way down the path, he whistled a little tune and looked on at the tilted tombstones which to him resembled a crowd of crooked teeth protruding from grassy gums. From the corner of his eye, he noticed a flitter off in the distance behind one of the taller grave stones. He stopped to have a look. His whistling trailed off as he narrowed his eyes and scanned through the trees and grave markers. The crooked tombstones stood still in the breezeless heat of day. He decided it was a trick of the light and continued on whistling as he walked. Moments later there was movement again, only this time it was closer. It was strange how quickly it had covered the distance from where he had seen it only a moment or two ago. The silent stones offered no clues so he kept on walking until he saw a giant Ceiba tree just outside the cemetery entrance several yards away. People in those parts believed that Ceiba trees were a kind of doorway for the dead. He had heard many tales of ghosts seen standing under a Ceiba. He had always scoffed at the notion of spooks and superstitions. He continued his approach without hesitation when beneath the shade and tucked inside the folds of the elephantine trunk a figure stepped forward. He stopped mid step as a quick ripple of fear shot up his spine. He felt his stomach drop and the hairs on his neck stand on end. Not wanting to give in to what he thought was irrational fear, he slowly continued on keeping his eyes on the figure as he walked.

As he drew nearer to the Ceiba, the figure stepped out from the shade. It was a woman who was very much of flesh and bone, not a ghost at all. She was wearing a dingy lace dress and a tattered straw hat with a wide brim that hid her eyes and nose. She waved him over slowly with a pale thin arm. Something inside made him take pause again. A voice, his own voice, told him to turn back. A conflict arose inside him between sense and the senses. The woman kept her head angled slightly down as she continued to beckon him. He couldn't be sure, but beneath the ragged edge of the brim were thin waxy lips unnaturally stretched into what he thought was a closed smile. She did not speak to him and he sensed that he should not speak to her. In fact, he sensed he should walk, no, run away. But he did not wish to be rude or appear afraid, so he slowly approached the woman. At first glance and in the shade of the Ceiba, she gave the illusion of being a much younger woman. Her pallid skin, petite build, and the youthful silhouette of her dress had misled him. As he neared her, he realized that she was very old. He had not noticed her wrinkled skin. It occurred to him that she also seemed somewhat blurry. He closed and opened his eyes several times trying to focus through the mottled sunlight filtering from the branches above. *This was an old woman.* It was clear to him now that she was very old. He chided himself for feeling any fear. The woman was more than likely in need of some assistance. With that he gave no second thought to the voice in his head, her abrupt appearance, or that he still had not seen her whole face. He walked straight up to her. With one skeletal claw she clamped down on his arm drawing him firmly against her frame. He was younger and more imposing than her, but she held him with a supernatural vice-like grip. With his free hand he tried to pry hers off, but a reflexive wave of repulsion made him withdraw it. The skin on her hand was a thin loose membrane. His fingers furrowed in it as if he were kneading soft dough. Beneath it he could feel the hard nubs of her knuckles. Her finger tips were blackened by soil that outlined her splitting yellow fingernails. He could tell she had been digging. He pulled away as hard as he could to escape her hold. The straight line of her mouth never wavered. She kept her head tilted down so that the brim of the hat continued to conceal

her eyes. The suspense of not knowing what they looked like roused a terror in him, and then, there was the smell. A loamy stench mingled with the sickly sweetness of rot.

"Let me go!" he cried.

She raised her head up and revealed the two blacks caverns that served as place markers for her eyes. He howled in sheer terror. She was not old, she was dead. She was a walking corpse in the light of day. He realized the permanent grimace of her mouth remained so because it was stitched in place by the undertaker. He tried to pull his face away from her, but she tightened her grip. He looked on in horrific disbelief as she raised her free hand to his face. She slipped one blackened finger into the outer corner of his right eye. There was a searing pain and pressure, so much pressure that it immobilized him. He felt the finger unplug muscles then hook behind his eyeball. He nearly fainted at the wet belch of his eye popping out of the socket. She placed the glistening red-tailed orb into one of the eyeholes in her face as he quietly sobbed. Tears streamed from both eyes. She removed the other eye. Once the deed was done she dropped him to the ground at the base of the Ceiba. He instinctively tucked into the long sloping folds at the base of the tree. He drew his knees to his chest and whimpered softly. His eyelids sagged like trouser hems that were too long. He braced for whatever else was next. It took a second or so for him to realize that she had walked away. She was making her way across the small country graveyard. She stopped at one grave in particular. The grass and soil were churned and clumped around a hole. Inside there were shards of wood easily splintered by seasons of rot. The name on the stone read *Marie.* He could see where she was going and everything she was doing. By some devilry he could see everything she did as if he were her. She trudged past the small clapboard chapel on the other side of the graveyard then exited.

It was dusk by the time she reached paved streets. She walked for many blocks. He could see houses he did not recognize and the startled expression on peoples faces as she passed them on the sidewalk under the amber glow of the street lamps. Finally, she arrived at a quaint looking house with gingerbread trim. She did not go up the front walk to the door. Instead, she made her way around to the back and slipped into an unlocked back door inside a screened porch. She moved with purpose suggesting she was familiar with the house. She went straight to a small bookcase in the sitting room. She pulled out a marquetry box from one of the shelves, tucked it under her arm then made her way down a long hallway. She stopped in the doorway of the room at the end. There was an old man asleep in bed. He laid there face up and mouth open. His breathing was shallow and labored. She watched him for a bit. When she had seen enough she exited the house and walked all the way back through the streets, back through the woods, to the graveyard. It was fully dark by the time she returned. When she reached the Ceiba, he could see his own body huddled against the trunk of the tree. He saw himself sit up and reach his arms out trying to feel around. The disconnect between his sight and his body was jarring. His face was a Greek mask of tragedy each eye an empty hole. He saw her pull out the box. She opened it. Inside was a book, the title of which he could not make out. She opened the book and the pages parted to reveal a flower. It had been pressed between the pages of the book. She pinned the desiccated relic of what was once a yellow rose to the shoulder of her moldy dress. She walked over and lifted him to her. He cowered in her grasp. She held his chin with one withered hand. With the other she plucked each eye out and returned them to each socket in his face. She released him and disappeared back towards the graveyard. He remained in a heap beneath the Ceiba for hours waiting for daylight- knowing, however, that daylight no longer guaranteed safety.

Days later after the man had recovered from the harrowing encounter in the graveyard, he was still haunted by what he witnessed. Attempting to find a reason for the strange events, he retraced the path the corpse had taken. He found himself at the front gate of the same quaint house with the gingerbread trim. There were several people coming and going. All were dressed in black. He had arrived during a wake. There was no doubt in his mind that the gathering of mourners was for the old man. Still curious, he walked in pretending to come pay his respects. There were people clustered around a table that had been laid out with an assortment of dishes. He shouldered past the grazing mourners by the table looking for a better vantage point of the room. He slid into a corner then looked around past the guests. He took in the room itself and realized he was in the same sitting room where the corpse had retrieved the box. In fact, he was leaning against the same bookcase. He glanced around quickly to make sure he wasn't being watched and then craned his head down to examine the contents of the shelves. He saw the gap left by the missing box. On the same shelf were several books. There were two well worn volumes of Shakespeare's works. He found volumes I and III. He surmised that Volume II must have been the book inside the wooden box that held the pressed corsage. He noticed a silver framed picture on the shelf just above. It was a young couple sitting on a giant cutout of a whimsical crescent moon with a cartoon face. It was the kind of keepsake picture taken at state fairs or tourist destinations. In the picture, the young man's arm hung relaxed around the girl's shoulders. She held his other hand between hers. The couple leaned into each other pressed cheek to cheek. Their happy beaming faces were full of youth and light. Though the photo was in black and white, the young man's eyes had a quality of clear glass giving the impression that his eyes were a very light blue. The young man was dressed smartly in his pressed shirt and slacks with his hair combed to one side and shiny from several splashes of hair tonic. The young woman had dark luminous eyes and her smile suggested she was having the time of her life. He lingered on her face sensing the moment of joy and love the photograph captured so distinctly. Then he noticed it. It was right there the whole time. The rose. The girl had a rose pinned to her dress. A shiver ran down his spine. He felt a piece of loose paper with his fingers on the back of the frame. He flipped it over. There were two ticket stubs and a scrap of paper taped to the back. Written on the paper in lovely feminine loops and tails it read:

Felix and Marie
Our first date.

Just then a woman walked up and startled him. He was afraid he'd been found out, but the woman didn't seem to mind that he was looking at the deceased's personal effects. Gently, she took the frame from him and regarded it while she wiped the glass with a handkerchief she'd been crying into. He stood there for an awkward moment. Then she sighed and explained without solicitation.

"That was their first date, " she said in revery. "It was a blind date. She carried a yellow rose so he would recognize her among all the other girls there that night. That was the night they fell in love. From then on they were never apart. They were married for 62 years. She passed away last Winter. He took to the bed shortly after. Today is the anniversary of that first date. I hope that they can find each other again." The woman clutched the frame to her chest and dabbed at newly formed tears in her eyes. The man placed a hand on her shoulder to comfort her.

"I'm sure they did," he replied.

Wetwood

Caleb found a rusty pocket knife in the tall grass at the edge of the park where he sometimes hung out after school. It wasn't a child's pocket knife. It was big enough for a grown hand. He kept it hidden from his parents, who would have confiscated it at once. That same day he carefully cleaned the rust off the blade and lock-back mechanism with oil he found in the tool shed. He knew better than to bring the knife to school, but that weekend he carried it with him wherever he went. His mother sent him to the market to pick up a few things she needed for supper. In the produce section, he carved little faces into the apples and other fruits and vegetables when no one was looking. In the dried goods aisle, he lifted the corners on bags of rice and beans and cut small holes in each then quickly set them back down. He watched in wait from the end of the aisle then snickered with glee as an old woman plonked a bag in her basket and unknowingly left a trail of rice as she shopped throughout the store. It delighted him to see the chaos he so easily caused in the store as another customer began to trail beans through the aisles. The manager's gruff voice barked over the P.A. system like a Sargent calling his troop to clean up the mess.

Two scrawny teens carrying a broom and dustpan scurried out from the stockroom. Their eyes were wide with confusion over where to begin. There was rice and beans everywhere. Caleb strolled out of the store without a care for the damage he caused.

Later that day he rode his bike to the park where he wanted to carve his initials into one of the picnic tables like the cool older kids did. He traced the blade over and over his first initial which he had to make with two short intersecting lines that looked like a V on its side. He was hunched over the table concentrating on the job when he saw a pair of work boots walk up and park next to him. He looked up to see the groundskeeper eyeing him. Caleb quickly hid the knife behind his back, but he knew it was too late.

He stiffened and his face heated as he waited for a scolding. He was certain the man was going to haul him off to call his parents. His mother and father would bicker about who's fault it was that he even had a knife and then they would take it from him. Instead the groundskeeper just told him he could carve all he wanted. He told him that all the old picnic tables were being replaced by new concrete sets at the end of the month. Then he went back to swapping out the full trash bags for empty ones. Caleb looked down at all his efforts and exhaled sharply in defeat. He sat at the picnic table scanning around for a suitable canvas, but every other structure on the playground was metal or concrete. He glanced down at the table and noticed the initials $F + D$ with a heart carved around. He remembered seeing someone carve a similar declaration into a tree. There were plenty of trees around and they wouldn't be replaced any time soon he thought. He snatched up the knife and ran off towards the tree line at the back of the playground. Beyond the park was a wooded area and beyond that were the railroad tracks.

He trudged through the narrow woods looking for just the right tree. Most of the trees on this side of the tracks were newer growth with slender trunks that were too green. He walked several yards down the tracks where he saw a colossal tree tucked back on the other side. He ran across the tracks to the tree. It was a grand and ancient Black Walnut. It towered as tall as a building with a crown that spread for yards around the trunk like a giant umbrella. Stepping into its shade he instantly felt the difference in temperature. It was several degrees cooler and the deeper beneath its branches he got, the cooler still and darker it became. He ran his fingers over the deep furrows of the bark as he strolled around the massive circumference of the tree. He surveyed the height of the trunk all the way up into its boughs and smiled. The mighty giant had stood there for who knows how many decades enduring nature and man. It was magnificent and pristine. He was struck with a sense of awe.

"Perfect," he whispered.

And with that Caleb pulled out the knife and began peeling away a section of bark from the majestic old tree. He cleared a patch the size of a bread plate and began to carve. The Walnut wood was denser and much more difficult to cut through than the picnic table, but he was determined. Again, he traced the same crude C into the bare wood. Over and over he plowed the blade into the trunk. He struggled even more with his last initial S which ended up as a zigzag. At one point the knife slipped and cut his thumb. Without anything to dress the wound, he simply sucked as much blood as he could, and continued to carve into the flesh of the knot. Blood droplets swelled from the cut and dripped down onto the wood. He smeared the blood into the cuts on the cleared patch of wood. The blood collected into the groves of his initials and made them standout. He liked how it looked so he squeezed his finger and rubbed more blood on the letters. He began to feel a gentle tap-tap on his back and something wet. He reached behind and felt the spot on his back. In the dappled rays of light beneath the branches, something black and sticky glistened on his fingers. He looked up but could not make out where the drip had come from. Assuming it was sap he shrugged and kept on butchering the exposed patch of wood and darkening the letters with his blood. When he was done, he stepped back and admired his handy work, pleased with himself. His shirt was soaked through at the spot just below his shoulder blade with the strange sap. The fabric was plastered to his skin and was beginning to itch. He pulled off the t-shirt and wiped his back and hands. He balled up the t-shirt and chucked it as though making a three pointer into a small hollow at the base of the trunk. He made a little fist pump and yelled, "Yes!" Then darted back across the tracks all the way to his bike at the park.

That evening Caleb was walking back to his room after a warm bath when the itch began again. He stopped in the hall to scratch, this time trying to approach it from below, but he could not contort his arm enough to reach. His mother, who was putting away a load of washing, saw him twisting his arms behind his back. She saw a bright red blemish.

"Oh, please scratch it! Please!" Caleb implored.

"No sir! And you shouldn't scratch it either. It could become infected," she warned him. "It might be a bug bite. If it gets any worse, you can forget about that camp out with your friends. "

She pulled him close to have a better look at the blotch. The skin at the site glowed like a fresh burn and was warm to the touch. At the center was a little dimple. It looked more like a small gouge. It did not exhibit the tell-tale bump of an insect bite. Still, she dragged him to the bathroom and dabbed it with a white cream she withdrew from the medicine cabinet. She wasn't sure what he had, but she told him the cream would prevent an infection and sooth the itch. She was right. The the itching stopped. She ruffled his hair then scolded him for keeping such a messy room.

"Make sure you clean that room of yours, or..." she started.

"I know! I know! Or I won't go on the camping trip." Caleb finished for her then shut the door to his room to end her nagging. On Friday as he was dressing in the morning for school, he felt the fabric from his pajama top drag across something rough on his back. He twisted his arm under so he could feel for it, but it was just out of his reach. It didn't hurt or itch and he was in a hurry to catch the bus. He pulled on a clean shirt and ran downstairs. That day after school he and some other boys were playing tag in the empty lot at the end of the street. The boys had been running back and forth for the better part of an hour in the hot afternoon sun. Caleb was red as a beet and his black

Batman t-shirt was drenched in sweat. He took it off and again three pointed it onto his backpack sitting on the seat of his bike. Elliot ran towards him to try to tag him. Caleb turned to run away. Elliot began to chase him but suddenly stopped.

"Hey, what's that on your back?" Elliot called out.

"It's just a rash." Caleb replied annoyed by Elliot's question.

"You have a hole on your back and it's dripping," replied Elliot with his face scrunched up in disgust.

Just then the other boys ran over to have a look. The reaction on their faces mirrored Elliots. Caleb became self-conscious. He went over to his bike and picked-up the t-shirt. He realized it was damp with more than just sweat. He smelled a whiff of something rotten. He sniffed the t-shirt and could smell his own sweat, but there was something more. It smelled of mold and vinegar. Caleb looked over at the boys who had continued to play without him. He pulled out the pocket knife from his backpack. The boys were busy running around. Caleb poked a hole into the back tire of Elliot's bike then rode away. When he reached the house he burst through the front door and ran past his father who was sitting in the living room. He ran upstairs to the bathroom. No matter how he twisted about he could not see the hole. He rummaged through a drawer next to the sink until he pulled out a hand mirror. He stood with his back to the bathroom mirror, then holding the small mirror to one side he finally saw what had horrified his friends. On his back was a red leaf-shaped hole several inches in length with a dark red edge all around it. It oozed a thick pale gray puss. His mind immediately went to his mother's warning. He could not show his mother. He did not want to miss the camping trip. He jumped into the shower hoping to wash away the ooze. Afterwards as he dried himself he examined the residue left on the towel. It was thick. He wrinkled his nose at the smell. Caleb riffled through the medicine cabinet for the first aid kit. He pulled out gauze and medical tape. He cut a square of the gauze using a small pair of scissors in the kit and placed pieces of the tape diagonally at each corner of the gauze. At the center of the gauze square he squeezed some of the cream

his mother had applied days earlier. Then via a careful orchestration between the two mirrors and his father's long handled luffa he applied the crude patch over the hole. He pressed his back against the wall to secure the patch in place then slipped back to his bedroom where he put on fresh clothes. During dinner he could barely manage to sit still. Although the hole did not itch it slowly dripped more of the smelly ooze down his back and into the waistband of his shorts. At one point his father sniffed at the meatloaf on his fork trying to figure out where the smell was coming from. After dinner Caleb redressed the wound and this time there was a shallow trench where the ooze had eaten path down his back. Neither the the hole nor the trench hurt so he plugged them both with several more layers of gauze. He returned to his room and began to play a video game, but he soon grew tired. He was exhausted. He slipped into bed and almost at once drifted into sleep. Throughout the night Caleb dreamed of the big Walnut tree dripping its sticky black sap onto him. Caleb dreamed of completely melting into the sap. He dreamed of ooze that ran from red to yellow then grey. He dreamed of sinking down into the soil beneath to the roots of the Walnut. As Caleb slept in his bed the hole oozed just like the sap in his dreams. As it oozed, his body slowly dissolved throughout the night until he was no more than a puddle of goo in his bed.

In the morning Caleb's mother entered his room after he had not come down for breakfast. He was no where to be found. The sheets on his bed were covered in grey goo and the room wreaked of rotten vegetation. She grew angry, believing that he had made the mess somehow then taken off early on his bike before anyone else woke up. Her anger intensified when she saw the knife poking out from under the bed. She was furious. She stomped downstairs to inform Caleb's father about the mess and the knife. They bickered about how to punish him whenever he returned home. They were completely unaware that Caleb had never left. Later, his mother would place the sheets into the washing machine, unknowingly rinsing away all that remained of Caleb.

Pumpkin Guts

Decades ago, in the curio shop of time, there occurred an incident so unimaginable, so horrifying and so bizarre that it left the small town where it all happened rattled for generations. Where and when the horrific events unfolded are of little consequence. It is the mystery of how and why it suddenly erupted one day that chilled every town folk to the core. What happened was far beyond comprehension and the inability to make sense of the horror became the very reason for their terror, for it presented other more worrisome questions. Can this happen again? How can we protect ourselves? Are we safe? The questions would echo throughout every council meeting, dinner table, barbershop, and any other congregation for years to come, until one by one the witnesses moved away, grew old, or began to think the whole thing had been a figment of the entire town's imagination. There had in fact been deaths, that part was true. And yet, as time ticked past, the story around those deaths became a foggy legend. The unimaginable, horrifying and bizarre event, however true, was regarded as a fantastical tale recounted less and less over the years. That supernatural event that once occupied every waking thought and nightmare of the townspeople slipped into the hole of oblivion. Which is ironic really, given that it all began in a deep hole.

I was old enough then to be able to remember the important details, but young enough to still be here now and recount them. The incident began in the outskirts and worked its way to a bloody climax in the heart of town. What I'm sharing with you now is a timeline, cobbled together, of the events that happened from start to finish as told to me from the folks that were there at each scene as well as what I saw with my own eyes.

It was early winter in the whistle-stop community. The end-of-year festivities had just begun. This was the happy part of winter with all the enchantments that made the long cold days bearable; the spooky fun of Trick-or-treating, gathering with family for Thanksgiving dinner, and the warmth of Christmas with its customary feelings of brotherly love. On the fringes of the scattered rural community, there was an old fish farm. The ponds had dried up a long time ago leaving a cluster of large holes inside which the townspeople dumped the unwanted scrap of their lives. The proprietor of the former fish farm turned dump was an odious man named Wade. Aside from dumping their oversized junk, no one visited Wade. For his part, he was fine with that.

Once in a while a truck would kick up a trail of dust along the dirt road leading to Wade's property to alert him someone was coming with a dingy sofa or a rusty appliance. Wade made decent money on those drop offs, but they were few and far between. No, Wade made his biggest earnings twice a year. The first was after the annual Harvest Festival when the town unceremoniously chucked hundreds of pumpkins used to decorate the main streets, government buildings, and shops not to mention all the porches garnished with the orange gourds. His other big payday was, of course, after Christmas. A forest of desiccated trees sometimes still wrapped in a helix of tinsel were tossed like fallen soldiers onto the bed of a pick-up and hauled out to Wade's fish farm. The farm became the final resting place of several years worth of discarded and forgotten pumpkins, Christmas trees and all sorts of holiday adornments. Once they had served their fleeting ornamental purpose, into a hole they went. To avoid the stench of rot the holiday cast-offs were always dumped in the dried basin known as Pond #12, which was upwind from the lopsided farmhouse Wade called home. It was out in #12 that the insidious fermentation began.

At some point, no one knows when or how, the contents of Pond #12 combined to create a kind of foul primordial sludge. Seasons of putrefaction, chemical off-gassing, mold, and weathering had spontaneously begot an insatiably ravenous creature. Somehow a living entity was born from the rotted mush of hundreds upon hundreds of pumpkins and Christmas trees. Wade, or what was left of him, was the first to be discovered shortly before the incident at the town's square. It was old Fred, the owner of the town's one gas station, who stopped by with a truck full of bald tires to dump. He found what was left of Wade and phoned Deputy Elwood. When Elwood arrived he traced the long streak of pumpkin entrails and muck leading from Wade's house straight to Pond #12. He deduced that something had pulled itself out of the pit and dragged along to the farmhouse where it made Wade its first victim. Elwood struggled to understand what his eyes were seeing. What kind of man or animal did this? Wade had been sitting in a cracked leather armchair flipping through a pulp fiction magazine. Whatever it was, it broke through the window behind the chair where Wade must have been taken with great speed. He'd been snatched right out of his boots, which were still on the floor before the armchair covered in the same goo that made up the streak. It was a mishmash of pumpkin innards, bits of bloody pulp, tree sap, and other unidentifiable bits and pieces. On the floor next to the chair, lay a ghoulish coincidence. Wade's, bodiless left hand, was still holding the magazine which was open to a story titled *The Thing at the Window*. Elwood and Fred took notice and exchanged a grim look, but neither remarked in the moment. The rest of the house was left undisturbed. The culprit doubled back until it came to an area across from a field. Beyond the field was a small patch of dense woods and farther beyond that in the direction of town were cow pastures belonging to Abe Hoke. The deputy,

Fred, and Abe tracked the streak to several puddles of what appeared to be the remains of half a dozen of Abe's cows. Abe wept openly when it appeared the thing had devoured his best girl, Constance. She was missing among the muck of bloody cow intestines, weird pumpkin shards and orange slime. Abe had doted on that cow like a first born child. He collected himself and insisted he join deputy Elwood and Fred to help destroy whatever had taken his beloved cow from him. From there, the streak had grown wider and thicker. It was growing with each meal. The trail wound through several other parcels of farmland leaving a wake of dead livestock and stunned farmers. Some had not even been aware of the carnage on their own land. Once it had eaten its way past the farms, the trail disappeared on the banks of a nearby river. The river served as the runoff for the town's storm drains. This thing was hungry and town would be the best place for its next meal. The deputy and the two men knew things were about to get worse. They had to try to warn the others. It was headed right for town.

Almost the entire population was gathered at the town square for the annual tree lighting ceremony. Every year all the children and teens performed at the start of the holiday season. The kindergarteners were dressed up as angels with halos made of silver pipe cleaners and paper wings tied to their backs with ribbon. They sang carols which sounded more like a box of howling kittens than a choir of angels. The older children put on short skits stumbling through their lines or played off key in the lopsided orchestra despite the band directors efforts. Still, it was a cherished event and just about everyone came out to enjoy the start of the Christmas season. The local lodge was selling hot chocolate and baked goods. All the prominent members of the community were in attendance. Gordy Howell the postmaster dressed up as Santa and collected change for the Salvation Army. Of course, Mayor Gilbert and his snobby wife, Lavinia, were present. She was sitting next to the podium upright and full of herself, wearing an extravagant hat that featured a whole stuffed partridge nestled in a ring of holly. Mrs. Peacock's kindergarten class was still on stage behind Mayor Gilbert waiting to sing another round of carols. That's where I was. I was as mad as a puffed toad. I remember that pipe cleaner halo was digging into my scalp and my mother had made me wear a pair of hand-me-down penny loafers from the church poor box that were a whole size too small. My toes were smooshed up inside and they pinched my feet all over. If it wasn't for Vern Marshall I would've hobbled off that stage and chucked those loafers right at my mother. Mrs. Peacock had stood Vern next to me so I could be a good influence on him. It didn't occur to her that it could work back the other way. The problem was Vern's favorite pastime was cramming his index finger two knuckles deep into his nose to dig out a ball of snot which he'd then flick at anyone within range. At age five, gross was my favorite kind of funny. Mrs. Peacock had unwittingly set the fox to sleep right inside the chicken coop. Vern shot me a wicked toothless grin as his finger almost completely disappeared up one nostril. He wiggled the finger around inside like he was searching in a cupboard when his beady eyes lit up and that evil grin crept further across his freckled face. Carefully he pulled out a giant snot ball big enough for the record books. He rolled it around between two fingers to prime it. He readied it right at the end of his thumb with his middle finger pulled back behind it as though making an o.k. sign. Then he pretended his arm was a gun turret. He positioned it slowly making mechanical gear noises as it moved. It was too much for me. I slapped my hands over my mouth to keep from bursting out laughing. His squinted eyes scanned around until he had locked the finger onto his target. My eyes followed the line of his finger straight to that chicken on Lavinia Gilbert's head. I couldn't hold it in any longer. I doubled over and exploded into laughter. My whole body shook and I completely forgot about the pinchy shoes and halo. I caught myself almost instantly. I slapped my hand back over my mouth and looked over to see if Mrs. Peacock had heard or seen me. It was too late. From off stage she shot me a look of fire that could melt the face off a marble statue. I withered under the twin laser beams of her eyes. Vern dropped his finger down as Peacock stormed over and snatched me off the stage by the ear. Mayor Gilbert was babbling on at the podium about the upcoming events. As Mrs. Peacock reprimanded me, I rubbernecked around the wagging finger she shook in my face. I wanted to watch the whole spectacle unfold. With Peacock gone Vern had brought his finger back up and realigned his sight. He gave a devilish wink and launched the rather sizable snot canon right at Lavinia who had just turned back to see what all the commotion was about. The mucus meteor had missed the chicken on her head and instead landed with a soft tap where it stuck on her cheek. At the sight of this I erupted into a geyser of giggles. The more I laughed, the madder Mrs. Peacock got. Lavinia looked up and held out an open palm. She thought it was rain. It was not. She reached up to her cheek and took hold of the glob. She stared at it confused. Lorraine Watts and Althea Gruber who were standing just behind Lavinia and who narrowly escaped the path of the snot rocket cried in unison, "Ewwwww! It's a booger!" Lavinia held it up to her eyes for a better look, her brows set like a pair of knitting needles, still not comprehending what had happened. A second passed and I could see her expression change like all the pieces of a puzzle flying together until her face twisted up in disgust. She held her arm out to get some distance between her face and the booger. She was shrieking like a cat with its tail caught in a door and flicking her hand about, but that booger wan't going anywhere. Mayor Gilbert was stunned into silence. The whole ceremony came to a halt. Even Peacock stopped reprimanding me and turned around to have a look. While Lavinia screamed and waved her hand furiously to rid herself of that booger, the unimaginable, horrifying, and bizarre incident occurred. One minute it was all hot cocoa and Christmas carols, and the next, we were running for our lives.

At first, witnesses thought it was an explosion of some kind. Some time just before 6:00 p.m., the creature burst through the large storm drain at Abbott's Place near the gazebo in the town's square. A thick geyser of stringy orange and white mingled with tree branches and broken glass ornaments thrusted through the drain opening and launched two stories up into the air. The heavy metal grate was flung up several feet as well and crashed on a nearby bench that had just been occupied by Mary Sweeting, the town's librarian. As she stood up to introduce the Kindergarten class who were about to sing "*O' Come All Ye Faithful*," the grate clonked on to the bench splintering the wood slats in half. The giant arm of goo swayed in the air back and forth. The townspeople waited for it to slap back down onto the pavement, but it did not. The amorphous blob remained upright despite giving no indication of any skeletal framework. It was at this point that people remember thinking it was a giant worm or snake. Everyone stood transfixed by the unfathomable spectacle before them, including Mayor Gilbert and Lavinia who still held that booger up high on the end of her finger. The creature held itself upright poised like a Cobra. Then a giant maw opened towards the top revealing it had a mouth. It unleashed a loud long bellowing cry that rattled the windows of all the nearby shops. The stench of rotted pumpkin flesh and sickening sweet pine caused some of the children to bring up their hot cocoa right on the stage. This was followed by a second or two of utter silence. From back in the depths of its horrid mouth came a *tinny* mechanical melody. It was a broken snow globe stuck in the lining of what appeared to be its throat. The first four notes of *"Joy to the World"* played slow and halted. Incredulous, everyone stood frozen with their mouths open. Then without warning the giant arm-like thing whipped down without mercy and snatched Mayor Gilbert and Lavinia right from the podium into its hideous mouth. The whole length of its form throbbed as the creature absorbed the couple. There were loud digestive sounds of pumping and sipping and grumbling. They had no time to react. As it slurped them both up the rest of the crowd broke into chaos. Parents and teachers grabbed children. My father, who had been in the audience with my mother, vaulted over several rows of chairs and threw me over his shoulder. Mama held tight to my baby sister and the four of us fled for our lives. I watched the mayhem from the back window of our station wagon as father drove like the very devil himself was on our heels. There were screams and the sound of clanging instruments dropping to the ground as people scurried. The cocoa station was knocked over leaving a mess of hot chocolate and baked goods everywhere, which where then trampled. Chocolate footprints faded out from the scene. Sheriff Harris tried to shoot the thing but it barely noticed as the bullets were simply absorbed. It was still busy digesting the mayor and his wife. In a matter of minutes while the couple was churned into pulp the town square had been vacated except for the Sheriff, deputy Elwood, Abe and Fred who had arrived just in time. Everyone else scattered to safety. The thing, which was still sticking out of the drain pipe, released a giant burp. Again there was another wave of putrid pumpkin and pine. As it twisted about, the items within it shifted inside. Some of them would appear on the surface of its oozing form. A glint of tinsel or the buckle from an old Santa suit jumbled together with shards of pumpkin shells and Lavinia's gaudy mangled hat. Then it would twist around some more and those things would sink inward and others would come to the surface. Next there was a clump of angel hair and a mad-looking paper maché jack-o-lantern that bobbed up and down in the stringy pumpkin goo like a buoy in the ocean. Suddenly, it rumbled and shook from top to bottom, then squeezed down into a mound. It stretched horizontally across the ground and began to slowly snake across the town square as it exited the drain. It was twenty feet long and as it moved it left behind a revolting trail of sludge. The Sheriff, his deputy, and the two men were directly in its path. Moving flat across the ground it was slow but when it reared up it could throw its weight to strike quickly. The group stood at the northeast corner of the square inching backwards slowly. On that corner was Fred's garage. Fred looked over at his station and got the idea that maybe they could set the thing on fire if they lured it towards the gas pumps. The group agreed and began to back up towards the station. The creature followed them. When they reached the sidewalk just in front of the garage, Fred broke off from the group and ran to the door of the station office where he frantically fumbled for his keys, keeping a lookout over his shoulder. Sensing they were up to something the thing stopped. It molded itself back into an arm and quaked again before opening its grotesque abyss of a mouth. It roared once again and the windows all around them shook. It was about to strike. The sheriff yelled out for the group to scatter and hide. It stretched upward into the sky then whipped down at Fred who cleared the doorway just in time. The creature slammed against the door with such force that it left a large dent in the metal door. Fred hid inside. He peered over the counter through the large plate glass windows. The monster swiveled it's giant head and mouth around looking to snatch up one of the others, but they had taken cover. In the scramble to hide the men separated from one another except for Abe and Deputy Elwood who, in their hurry dove under the empty rickety fruit stands just outside of Vogels Grocery Store. Sheriff Harris was hiding just outside the gas station under Pete Sadowski's ice cream truck. He laid flat beneath the box truck which had a giant fiberglass replica of a Neapolitan triple scoop welded on top. None of them could move or call out to the others for fear of giving away their position. Stretched up tall as it was the creature was too quick. It was too dangerous. The sun had set leaving each one of them in the dark to watch the monster from their hiding spots. The thing seemed to glow an eerie orange beneath the yellow light of the sodium lamp posts. The empty streets stirred a sense of dread in each of the men as thoughts of not making it out alive began to sink in. A loud rumbling sound like that of a very large hungry stomach echoed from the creature. It was starving and eager for another meal. The giant opened its mouth again and roared angrily. It released more waves of stench. The men held their breath at the tangy smell of rotting vegetables and stomach bile that permeated the air. It swiveled around searching. Under the fruit stands, Abe could no longer bare the pain from crouching for so long. His knees were on fire. He tried to shift his weight as quiet as he could but he accidentally pushed up the underside of an empty crate which made a loud thump when it came back down. The creature reacted and turned towards the sound. The sheriff and Fred knew they had to do something to help them. The fruit stands were no protection. Inside the gas station, Fred had an idea. He grabbed a flashlight from under the counter. He had to try to communicate his idea to the sheriff and fast. With the monster craned away from the gas station Fred pointed the light at the sheriff and turned it on and off in long and short bursts. The sheriff understood that the flashes were morse code. From across the intersection Fred could see the shear terror in the eyes of the two men. There were two rows of stands on the East corner of Vogels and a third on the Southside facing Fred's garage where Abe and the Deputy huddled together. The creature whipped down at one of the stands on the East corner. It's cavernous mouth landed short of the stand and instead slammed hard onto the pavement leaving a large splotch of orange goop. It roared and gurgled furiously. It was wild with hunger. It whipped down again this time it landed on the stand leaving only shards of wood and metal. With each strike, the men could feel the ground quake beneath them. The Sheriff had seen Fred's message and understood the plan. Fred had a better view of the overall scene. The sheriff waited for his signal. Having destroyed the other two stands, the creature swiveled around and reared up in the direction of Abe and Deputy Elwood. Fred flashed the light at the sheriff. The sheriff rolled out from under the truck, jumped inside, and switched on the P.A. system. *Pop Goes the Weasel* filled the still night air and the creature stopped and whipped its long neck around. The sheriff jumped out of the truck and bolted towards the the gas station where Fred held the door open. The monster snapped down and clamped onto the triple scoop on top of Pete's truck. It wrapped it's mouth around and tried to churn it into a meal. *Pop Goes the Weasel* slowly came to a halt as the creature ate the speakers. Abe and Elwood saw their chance to run. The men took off towards the train depot down First street. Elwood, still a young man, ran fast without looking back. He assumed Abe had kept up, but Abe was much older and those bad knees were taking their time to limber up after crouching for so long. He was just past the intersection when he tripped over the pile of debris from the broken fruit stands. He landed hard onto the pavement. By the time Elwood turned around it was too late to help Abe. The monster, furious, had thrown up the fiberglass ice cream sending it crashing through the windows of Vogels. It spotted Abe sprawled on the street. It reared up again like a Cobra and swayed from side to side over him. Abe closed his eyes and curled up into a ball. He waited to be swallowed whole. A moment passed and nothing. A low gentle clang from yards away had drawn the creature's focus straight ahead past Abe. As the creature hovered, Elwood crouched down low and snuck back to Abe. They kept their eyes on the thing. It appeared to recognize the sound. Elwood helped Abe up and the two men hid in a nearby alley. From the gas station, Fred and the sheriff could see the thing shrink down into a mound and then slowly move down First street towards the train tracks where it sprouted again into a tower of ooze. Off in the distance came the sound of the 6:30 express freight that whizzed by every evening on its way to the city. Abe and Elwood peeked out from the alley and Fred and the sheriff cautiously crept out of the station to the intersection. They followed the creature's site line. There she was, the focus of the monster's attention. It was Abe Hoke's best girl, Constance. He tried to call out to her, but was quickly muzzled by Elwood. She had managed to escape the creature in the pasture and wandered away. Somehow she ended up by the train tracks across from the depot. The bell around her neck gently clanging as she grazed on the grass alongside the tracks. The men realized what was about to play out. But, would it work? The timing had to be right. And then there was the question of whether or not the impact would have any effect since bullets had already failed. The

creature seemed to remember the cows it swallowed earlier that day. Grumbling churning digestive sounds arose from the arm. Ravenous, it bellowed. The creature lunged at the heifer who was too busy grazing to notice she was about to be a burger and a shake for the creature. The whistle sounded loudly as the train conductor announced its approach. At the sound of all the commotion, Constance trotted off. The creature had no understanding of the mechanical beast headed straight toward it. It knew nothing of inertia. It was about to find out. As the giant arm reached across the tracks to consume the cow, the train slammed into it. The creature exploded in a gruesome and spectacular display. Orange goop, rotted pumpkin shards, and pine needles splattered over everything as far back as Fred's garage. The men were coated in the foul slime. The train conductor never saw the creature and the train continued barreling down the track on its way to deliver its cargo. The townspeople were left cleaning the creature's strange innards for weeks afterwards. Constance was hailed a local heroine. Abe pampered her till she died at the remarkable (for a cow) age of twenty-five. All the ponds at Wade's were filled in and eventually the land was sold off and turned into a strip mall.

Our family moved away as soon as possible like many others had done. Years ago I was passing through on my way to the city. I decided to check in on the old town. A great deal had changed, but so much of it was still there. It was like running into someone you haven't seen in a long time. Their hair could be different. Maybe they put on some weight, but their eyes and smile were the same. I was strolling past the elementary school. The very elementary school I once attended. It was recess and the children were all out playing in the schoolyard. Some were on the swings while others tossed a ball around. The sound of children laughing, screaming, and chanting children's rhymes filled the noon air. It was a happy familiar kind of sound. I was wrapped in my memories as I was about to cross the street when I heard it. I heard the word "pumpkin". Of course I've heard the word a million times over, but not here, not in this town. I stopped short and was instantly drawn back to that horrid nightmare day. I listened more intently, and then I heard it all. The creature had not only been immortalized in the humblest of ways, it had been given a name. It had become the folk villain of a schoolyard rhyme. A legend. A cautionary tale to be sung on the playground and passed along by generations of children like so many other horrible events before that were recorded as rhyme. Just like *Ring Around the Rosie* retells the grim realities of the plague, the unimaginable horrifying and bizarre incident that happened in our little town lived on in rhyme.

"Sticky, slimy, slippery dee
Pumpkin Guts is coming for me
Sticky, slimy, slippery goo
Pumpkin Guts is coming for you!"

About the author

Cuban-American, D. B. Albiza, is a life long fan of horror and all things scary. As a former middle school teacher for over twenty-five years she loved to dream up tales of fright to entertain her students. When she is not writing she and her husband enjoy listening to records and spending time with the lovable crew of pets they share a home with.

About the illustrator

Elizabeth Quiñonez is a Nicaraguan-American Concept Artist and Illustrator currently residing in Miami, FL. She has had the opportunity to create concept art for video games, album cover art for local musicians, and book illustrations. She has a deep interest in Japanese history and culture and is currently finishing her degree in Asian Studies with a concentration in Japanese Language.

A note from me

So? Did you enjoy the book? Did the stories creep you out? Did you like the illustrations? Did they unnerve you? If so, let me know, because your voice matters. Yes you, sitting there in class or in your room or wherever. Your opinion matters to me. Please take a quick moment to leave an honest review. It would mean the world to me. Thanks for your time.

Scan to leave a review.

. . .